624

COPING WITH

ABSENT PARENTS

Mary Colson

Chicago, Illinois

www.heinemannraintree.com

Visit our website to find out more information about Heinemann-Raintree books.

To order:

☎ Phone 888-454-2279

🖳 Visit www.heinemannraintree.com to browse our catalog and order online.

Edited by Louise Galpine and Laura Knowles
Designed by Richard Parker
Picture research by Liz Alexander

Originated by Capstone Global Library Ltd
Printed and bound in China by
    Leo Paper Products Ltd

15 14 13 12 11
10 9 8 7 6 5 4 3 2 1

Library of Congress Cataloging-in-Publication Data
Colson, Mary.
  Coping with absent parents / Mary Colson.
      p. cm. — (Real life issues)
  Includes bibliographical references and index.
  ISBN 978-1-4329-4760-6 (hc)
  1. Latchkey children. 2. Children of working parents.
I. Title.
  HQ777.65.C65 2011
  306.874—dc22
2010020920

Acknowledgments
The author and publisher are grateful to the following for permission to reproduce copyright material: Alamy pp. **17** (© World Religions Photo Library), **24**, **25** (© axel leschinski), **26** (© Simon Belcher), **27** (© Catchlight Visual Services), **29** (© Spencer Grant), **30** (© PhotoAlto), **31** (© Myrleen Pearson), **33** (© Radius Images), **35** (© Bubbles Photolibrary); Corbis pp. **4** (© Heide Benser), **12** (© JGI/Jamie Grill/ Blend Images) **14** (© Pascal Deloche /Godong), **18** (© Heide Benser); Getty Images pp. **7** (Seth Joel), **9** (Jose Luis Pelaez Inc/Blend Images), **16** (Fred Morley/Fox Photos), **19** (Joe Raedle), **22**, **23** (Tanya Constantine/Digital Vision), **39** (Barry Austin/Digital Vision), **41** Alistair Berg/Digital Vision), **20** (Justin Sullivan); Photolibrary pp. **8** (Charlie Schuck/ Uppercut Images), **37** (Medicimage), **43** (Cade Martin/ Uppercut Images); **38** (Corbis); Press Association Images p. **11** (Charlie Neibergall/AP); Shutterstock pp. **5** (© Monkey Business Images), **15** (© EDHAR)

"Distressed texture" design detail reproduced with permission of iStockphoto/© Diana Walters.

Cover photograph of teenage boy looking out of a window reproduced with permission of Corbis/ © Tom Grill/Tetra Images.

Quotation on page 14 extracted from menassat.com, a website published by Arab Images Foundation. Quotation on page 34 extracted from the Findings *How Primary School Children Cope with Family Change* published in 2002 by the Joseph Rowntree Foundation. Reproduced by permission of the Joseph Rowntree Foundation.

We would like to thank Anne Pezalla for her invaluable help in the preparation of this book.

Every effort has been made to contact copyright holders of material reproduced in this book. Any omissions will be rectified in subsequent printings if notice is given to the publishers.

In order to protect the privacy of individuals, some names in this book have been changed.

Disclaimer
All the Internet addresses (URLs) given in this book were valid at the time of going to press. However, due to the dynamic nature of the Internet, some addresses may have changed, or sites may have changed or ceased to exist since publication. While the author and publisher regret any inconvenience this may cause readers, no responsibility for any such changes can be accepted by either the author or the publisher.

CONTENTS

Stay safe on the Internet!
When you are on the Internet, never give personal details such as your real name, phone number, or address to anyone you have only had contact with online. If you are contacted by anyone who makes you feel uncomfortable or upset, don't reply, tell an adult, and block that person from contacting you again.

Any words appearing in the text in bold, **like this**, are explained in the glossary.

Introduction

There are many reasons why parents and family members may be absent for a while. Sometimes work can take parents away, or they may be called to serve their country in the military. They might become sick, or decide to separate from each other. You may need to live with other adult caregivers if your parents have problems coping.

When your parents are absent, you will experience a range of emotions. It is important to remember that parents often feel exactly the same way as children do when they have to be apart from their families.

Sometimes your parents' jobs mean they cannot be there for you all the time.

CASE STUDY

Many jobs do not involve working a standard working day, from 9 a.m. to 5 p.m., Monday to Friday. For example, the emergency services need workers around the clock, as do the military, power stations, and hospitals. Corrie's dad, Richard, is a police officer who works evening and night **shifts**. "I try hard not to miss important events like school concerts, but I can't always change my shift," he says. Corrie wishes her dad were at home more "to help me with my homework and just to talk to."

How this book can help

Coping without your parents is never easy, but it is sometimes necessary. Whatever the reason for your parents' absence, this book will show you ways of coping and let you know whom you can talk to and contact if you need support.

Enjoying being together and remembering happy times will help you to cope when you are apart.

Working Away from Home

When working away from home, a parent may be absent on either a short-term or long-term basis. Short-term absence is when a parent is away from home for anything from a few days up to a few weeks. Long-term absence can mean you do not see your parent for months at a time.

Your parent might have to travel to work each day, or he or she might have chosen a well-paid job away from home in order to make the family's **financial** future more secure. This means your parent might only be home on weekends. There are some jobs that can only be done far away from home, such as jobs in the offshore gas and oil industries.

Counting days

If your parents are not at home, it is important to talk to the adults who are taking care of you about how you are feeling. Short-term absence always has an end in sight. You can count down the days to when your parent is home again. Some children make calendars and cross off the days as a way of coping.

BEHIND THE HEADLINES

Over 50,000 people work on oil rigs and gas platforms in the Gulf of Mexico. Many people also do this work in the Arctic Ocean off Alaska. Oil rig workers usually work one month on and then one month off. Working like this means that workers are at home and on **paid leave** for half the year.

Even if your parent is absent for weeks at a time, you can still keep in touch through phone calls, texts, and emails.

Irregular hours

Many companies operate "flex time," which allows people to manage their working time to suit them. For example, your parent may work extra hours on a weekday in order to not work as much on the weekend. That way, they can spend more time with you on the weekend.

Many jobs involve travel away from home and irregular hours. If your parent works in the travel industry or the military, he or she may often be away from home for short or long lengths of time. Long-haul pilots, flight attendants, and people in the merchant navy will all travel away from home with their work.

Some jobs involve travel away from home. It can feel good to be reunited after a long absence.

Online!

The best way to cope is to contact your parent while he or she is away. Modern technology helps you to communicate really easily. When you are missing your parents, just remember TEST: Text, Email, **Skype**, or Tweet!

When parents are absent, you might spend time with other relatives.

CASE STUDY

Sometimes parents take on extra work in the evenings or at night to boost their earnings. They might work in a restaurant or a warehouse, tutor students, or grade tests and papers. This means they will not be around for dinner or bedtime every night. Jenny, an English teacher, grades school papers in the evenings during January and June. She says, "My three kids spend a lot of time with their grandma in those months, but they love it. They get really spoiled and the extra money pays for a family summer vacation."

A change of plan

It is sometimes very difficult to tell what will happen in life. You might have made plans to spend a wonderful day with your parents, but then one of them is suddenly called away because of work.

Firefighters, lifeboat crew, and doctors are just some of the people who might have to suddenly cancel plans and go to work. They are often **on call** in the evenings and on weekends and must respond if needed. Members of the military can also be called away suddenly (see page 18–23).

Unexpected and sudden absence can have a real impact on family plans. It can even disrupt special occasions such as birthdays and holidays. Unfortunately, these absences cannot always be avoided, since emergencies can happen at any time.

Sometimes firefighters are specialists in certain types of industrial fire, such as oil rig fires. These fires can take a long time to put out or control, and the firefighters can be away for a few weeks. This happened in 2010 with the Gulf of Mexico oil spill. Some emergency workers were away from home for weeks as they dealt with the crisis.

Fun times ahead

Coping with sudden change can be difficult, especially if it means missing out on something fun or special. It is important to remember that your parent is doing very important work and may even be saving lives. Feel proud of what your parent does, and when he or she comes home you can make a new plan together.

DISCOVERER
ENTERPRISE

Emergency workers battled to put out the
fire on the Deepwater Horizon oil rig in the
Gulf of Mexico in April 2010. Thousands more
workers traveled to the area to try to clean
up the oil spill.

Living Away from Home

Parents have to decide what is best for their whole family. This might mean they make the difficult choice to live in a different country from their children for **financial** reasons, career opportunities, or even safety reasons. How can this affect you, and what can you do to cope?

In a parent's absence, it is sometimes grandparents who look after the children.

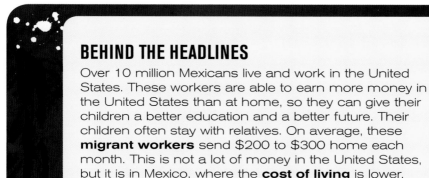

BEHIND THE HEADLINES

Over 10 million Mexicans live and work in the United States. These workers are able to earn more money in the United States than at home, so they can give their children a better education and a better future. Their children often stay with relatives. On average, these **migrant workers** send $200 to $300 home each month. This is not a lot of money in the United States, but it is in Mexico, where the **cost of living** is lower.

If a parent lives **abroad**, he or she might be absent for many months at a time. Your parent will be working hard to send money home or to get established in the new country so that you can come and settle there, too. Regular phone calls can help to bridge the distance. If you find talking on the phone difficult, write a list of all the things you have done so you don't forget to say them. Ask your parent questions about his or her daily routine, too, so you get an idea of what life is like in the new country. Making a scrapbook all about the country your parent is living in is a good idea, too. If you move there as well, it will help to prepare you for being in a new place with a different **culture**.

Online!

Millions of people all over the world write online diaries called "blogs." Writing down how you're feeling can help to make things clearer. Your parent could also keep a blog when he or she is away so that you could read each other's. Ask an adult to help you get started and to supervise your Internet use.

Career development

In some areas of work, such as medicine, construction, and international business, working abroad for a period of time is an opportunity to advance a career. Sometimes working abroad provides better pay and more responsibility. When your parent comes home, he or she will be more likely to get a better job. These positions abroad are often for a fixed period of six or twelve months.

CASE STUDY

The Gulf state of Dubai employs an estimated 500,000 foreign construction workers, many of whom come from South Asian countries such as India, Pakistan, Bangladesh, and Nepal. These workers earn more money in Dubai than they can at home, so they leave their families behind and send money back to them. Life is difficult for workers in Dubai because they do not see their families very often. Raj Kundar left his home in Nepal to earn money for his two children to have a good education. He said, "Almost all Nepalese have the same reasons for coming here. I go back to Nepal every year or 15 months."

Foreign construction workers have come to Dubai to earn more money than they could in their home countries.

Online!

Using the Internet to see maps and images of where your parent is working will help you to understand more about his or her daily life. On various map websites, you can find a street view of where your parent lives. Remember to always ask an adult to help you search the Internet.

Finding out about where your parent is working will help you feel closer while he or she is away from home.

Seeking safety

Sometimes parents decide that their family would be safer or have more freedom living in another country. Leaving one country and going to live in another because of **persecution** is called seeking **asylum**. Children are sometimes sent ahead of their parents to escape what their parents see as a dangerous situation. At first they might stay with relatives or friends in the new country.

BEHIND THE HEADLINES

Kinder is the German word for children. Between 1938 and 1939, over 10,000 Jewish children were sent by their parents on trains from Nazi Germany to safety in the United Kingdom. They went without their parents and were put in **foster care** with British families or they lived in children's homes. In 1939 World War II began and the Nazi leader Adolf Hitler ordered the murder of millions of Jews. As a result, most of the children who escaped to the United Kingdom never saw their parents again.

German Jewish children were sent abroad for their own safety.

CASE STUDY

If you go to live in a new country, there will be many changes to adapt to. There might be a new language to learn and a new culture to understand. Clothes and food might be different, too. This can be scary, but exciting. Youlia and Dmitri moved from Russia when they were young. At first they did not speak any English. "Children at school were friendly but we couldn't understand what they were saying! Within a few months, we could speak English and we made proper friends."

Most people quickly make new friends in school.

Military Service

Military families have to cope with situations that are often beyond their control. They might have to move bases, or even countries, because of their military jobs. One of the most challenging situations, both for you and your parents, is when your father or mother is sent for military service and must be away from home. You might feel frightened and sad, but you can be proud of what your parent is doing.

When people join the army, navy, or air force, they swear an **oath of allegiance** in which they promise to defend and serve their country. Being in the armed forces means that sometimes a person goes away on a **tour of duty** that can last from a few weeks to a few months. So, how do you keep in touch when your parent is away?

Writing a letter will help keep in touch with your parent. It is sometimes easier to write your thoughts and feelings down rather than say them.

Letters from home mean a lot to people working away from home in the military.

BEHIND THE HEADLINES

Thousands of parents are in the U.S. armed forces. Since 2001 many have been involved in wars around the world, particularly in Afghanistan and Iraq. This takes them a long way away from their families. The U.S. Postal Service operates a special "Free Mail" service for service members posted in many areas overseas. This allows service members to send personal letters back to the United States at no cost. Family members in the United States must pay postage when they send letters or packages to family members serving overseas, however.

Time to talk

If your parent has to go away on military duty, you may be anxious or worried. Talking with your parent before he or she leaves might help to show that you are both feeling sad and upset. You can also discuss all the ways you can keep in contact while your parent is away.

If your parent is away on a tour of duty, you can keep in touch by texts, emails, phone, and **Skype**.

CASE STUDY

Isobel's father is in the navy. In April 2008 he was sent to serve in the Persian Gulf for six months. Isobel explains her feelings while he was away:

"The first time my dad went away I was scared for him. On the television, I saw soldiers in Iraq and Afghanistan who were getting injured and killed and I thought that was what it would be like for my dad. My main concern was that he was going to get hurt and that I wouldn't see him again. Keeping busy on weekends and trying not to worry were the main ways of coping.

To keep in touch with him while he was away we mainly used Skype since we could see each other, which was good. He also called every night. I missed him, but keeping in touch regularly helped us cope and made it easier for when he came home again."

Online!

In Alabama over 100 libraries have been equipped with computers, Internet access, and video web cameras as part of the "Connecting Families" program. The program allows military families to use Internet software so they can make video calls to their loved ones overseas. It is difficult when families are thousands of miles apart, but being able to see each other on the computer screen helps to ease feelings of sadness.

On call

In many countries, the military assists in times of emergency. When Hurricane Katrina flooded New Orleans, Louisiana, in 2005, the U.S. Army, Navy, and Air Force were called up to organize and lead the enormous rescue operation. There is usually no warning before a natural disaster, so sometimes a military parent might have to leave home with very little notice. If your parent is called away to help in this way, you know that your parent's special skill will help people in need. Perhaps your mom or dad is saving lives. Be proud of the good work your parent is doing. You will be together again when the emergency situation is under control.

BEHIND THE HEADLINES

On January 12, 2010, a deadly earthquake struck the Caribbean country of Haiti. Within a few days, thousands of military men and women from many different countries were sent to help. In an emergency, every second counts, and lives can be lost because of delays. The military works quickly to help people.

Online!

If your parent has to go away suddenly in the line of duty, it is easy to keep in contact using new technology on the Internet. **Social networking sites** can help your family to keep in touch with each other. On some websites, you can send short, instant messages, so it feels as though you are really talking. Remember only to use these websites under the supervision of an adult.

Social networking sites make international communication easy and quick.

Addiction and Social Problems

Just like you, your parents can sometimes have personal problems. Usually they can cope, but occasionally they cannot. If this happens, life can become very difficult for everyone.

Some people might try to make themselves feel better by **gambling**, drinking, or even taking drugs. This may make them unable to be a good parent to you. If this happens, **social workers** can become involved.

Drinking a lot can be a sign that a person is not coping and needs help.

Here to help

Social workers visit homes and talk to families going through difficulties. They decide whether parents are able to take care of their children properly. They can help arrange support such as **counseling**, medical assistance, and housing.

WHAT DO YOU THINK?

You might worry that telling someone about your parent's problems will mean your family will be split up. But what's the best thing to do?

Why you might not want to tell an adult...	Why you should....
I'll be taken away to live with strangers.	Splitting up families is a last resort. Supporting families and keeping them together is the first priority.
I'll never see my mom/dad again.	If your parent cannot take good care of you, you may move with relatives or be placed into **foster care** for a short time. This gives your parent a chance to sort out problems and get better.
It will get better on its own.	The situation might improve on its own, but it will get better much quicker, and your family life will return to normal faster, if your parent gets the help he or she needs.

Living in foster care

If a social worker decides a parent is not able to care for his or her child properly, this may lead to the child living with someone else. The first choice is another family member, but if this isn't possible, the child will live with foster parents or in a children's home.

Parents who can't cope can leave their children feeling isolated and lonely.

Living in a children's home

Children's homes are usually run by charities and the children are looked after by paid staff. The children still go to school and can join in local activities. The thought of living in a home or foster family can be scary, so try talking about it to a teacher or another adult you trust.

CASE STUDY

A foster family is not a permanent family, but it is a family that will care for **vulnerable** children, sometimes at short notice. If, after some time, the social worker decides that the birth parents still cannot care for their children properly, the children may be **adopted** by new parents.

Robert and Michael went to live with foster parents because their mother was struggling with drug addiction and **financial** problems. They lived with their foster parents for two years before they were adopted. They are now very happy in their new family.

Foster parents do their best to listen and make things easier for you.

Parent in prison

If your mom or dad is sent to prison, it can put a strain on family relationships. It might make you feel guilty and ashamed, frightened and confused—all at once. You might struggle to understand the crime your parent committed, or find it difficult to get used to your parent not being at home anymore.

Visiting hours

If your parent goes to prison, you can still visit and stay in contact. All prisons have visiting hours when you can arrange to see your parent. Most prisons in the United States have a visitation room where you meet up with your parent. If you cannot visit in person, you can talk to your parent on the phone or write letters.

Counseling

Talking to a teacher or school **counselor** can help you to understand your feelings. You might find it hard to tell your friends or you might worry about being bullied. But the counselor will listen and give advice about how to cope. If you are feeling isolated and lonely, the counselor can tell you about support groups like Big Brothers Big Sisters, which is a nationwide **mentoring** organization. Young people are given a mentor whom they can talk to, hang out with, and have fun with.

An estimated 1.5 million U.S. children have a parent in prison. Phone calls, letters, and emails are all allowed and are important to use.

Separation and Divorce

All relationships are complicated and go through good and bad patches. Most adult couples argue sometimes, just like brothers and sisters do. But if your parents argue a lot, this can be upsetting for the whole family. If your parents' relationship is going through difficulties, they will be sad and maybe angry, too, but try to remember that they are not angry with you.

Sometimes it is not possible for parents to stay together.

CASE STUDY

Max's parents separated when he was 10 years old. He remembered, "They didn't argue much but they just weren't very happy. My mom cried sometimes. When they split up, they were friends again. We see Dad most weekends."

Parents can't always stay together

If the difficulties between your parents are too big for them to deal with, they might decide to separate. Separation usually means one parent will move out of the family home. This decision is not an easy one, and it will bring changes for the whole family.

A separation might last for a few weeks or months, or it could be forever. Getting used to seeing only one parent for part of the week can be difficult. It is important to remember that you are not alone. Everyone in the family will be feeling sad and confused, just like you. Writing a diary or talking to your parents or a grandparent will help you figure out your feelings.

It's good to talk to your friends. They will make you feel better.

A legal agreement

A divorce is a legal agreement that ends a marriage. A couple that wants to divorce will hire their own lawyers to draw up divorce papers. These papers contain information including which parent you will live with and how often you will see the other parent.

A judge decides which parent is best able to take good care of you. In some cases, one parent may lose **custody**, which means that you live with your other parent. This might be for **financial** or social reasons. After these important decisions have been made, both parents sign the papers and, after the judge has agreed to the divorce, it becomes **legally binding**.

Agreeing

Parents usually try to do what they think is best. But the divorce process can be very emotional, and sometimes parents cannot agree on how to manage the family, house, and money. A divorce **mediator** can help a divorcing couple to work through unresolved conflict. This helps them to get through the divorce process and continue to be good parents afterward.

Support network

Relatives, friends, and teachers are all around to offer help and support. If you can't talk to either of your parents, you might find it helpful to talk about your feelings with one of your relatives. You might think the separation and divorce is all your fault, but it never is. You might also think that you could have done something to stop the divorce from happening, but that is never true, either. Separation and divorce are about your parents' relationship with each other. It is not about how they feel about you.

Deciding to divorce is never easy. A lawyer will carefully go through the divorce papers with a couple who are separating.

Different homes

Becoming used to seeing less of one parent takes time. You might have to move to a new town, and you may have to adjust to a new school and new friends.

Many children find that once the divorce is finalized, things calm down a little and parents are much happier. Once the stress of the divorce is over, all the family members can start enjoying life again.

CASE STUDY

When Elise was 10, her parents divorced. She says, "There's nothing children can do [if parents split up]. There's no point getting involved because it might make it worse." She says the best thing to do is "try to … get on with normal life."

New beginnings

One or both of your parents may eventually find new partners and perhaps get married again. If their new partners have children already, you will have a whole new stepfamily to meet! This can be strange at first, and it may mean having to share your room or belongings with your new family. Everyone will be making changes, and it is important to all get together and talk about how you are feeling. Talking about the changes will help you feel that you have some control and that your feelings are important. Once you are used to the new situation, you might find that your stepbrothers or stepsisters become your new best friends.

It will take time to get used to new living arrangements.

Coping with Illness

Living with a parent who has a long-term illness can be difficult in many ways. Perhaps you worry about whether your parent is going to be all right, and you feel anxious or sad, and sometimes lonely. Your parent may not be able to do all the things you have done together in the past, or go to special events with you, and so adjustments have to be made. You might need to help out more at home, such as keeping your bedroom neat or putting groceries away. Remember that there are ways to cope.

Speak up

Parents try to protect their children, so they may pretend everything is fine even when it is not. Having to guess what is wrong will only confuse you and make you feel worse, so instead speak up and let your mom and dad know that you want the truth. Speaking up will show your parents that you can cope with serious information.

Staying with relatives

If your parent has to go to the hospital, you might go to stay with relatives. Before you go, pack a bag with some familiar things. These will remind you of home while you are away. Looking at family photos can also help, as can little objects, such as vacation souvenirs, that tell a family story and remind you of happy times.

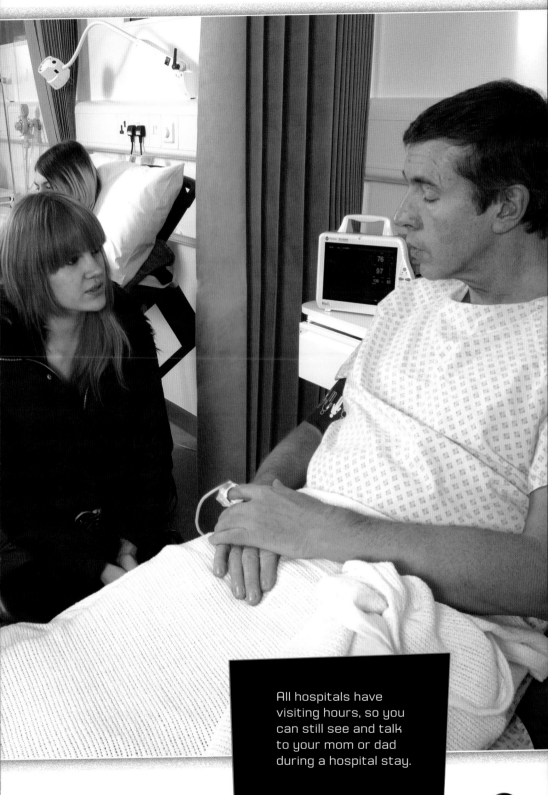

All hospitals have visiting hours, so you can still see and talk to your mom or dad during a hospital stay.

The child caregivers

Caring for a sick parent takes a lot of time and energy. Across the world, millions of children stay at home to care for a sick parent every single day. They keep the household going by doing the shopping, cleaning, paying bills, and taking care of their sick mom or dad. Unfortunately, children who do this can miss out on many opportunities. They might miss school or not have as many close friends as other children their age.

While sick parents are not actually "absent," they are often unable to meet a child's ideas of what a parent normally does. Sometimes this means that the child must do what the parent usually would. If you are in this situation, there are people and organizations that can help. Ask an adult relative or teacher to help you look on the Internet for support.

It is not easy to take care of younger siblings or do a parent's job, but there are organizations that can help.

Try not to feel guilty when you are out playing and having fun with your friends. It's okay to think about something else for a while.

BEHIND THE HEADLINES

It is estimated that the number of children who care for a sick relative in the United States is 1.3 to 1.4 million. The child caregivers help their relative with washing, dressing, and taking medicine as well as doing household tasks such as shopping, cooking, and cleaning. These are jobs that an adult would normally do, and doing them leaves child caregivers without much time for themselves.

Coping with Absent Parents

Throughout your life, your parents will occasionally be absent for short or long periods of time, for all sorts of different reasons. It might be anything from a late **shift** at work to a long-term contract **abroad**. It could be for social or health reasons, or it might be because your parents have separated.

Support networks

Parents have to make decisions about what they think is best for the whole family. In some situations, those decisions are beyond their control. The important thing to remember is that you have ways of coping. Brothers, sisters, grandparents, aunts, and uncles are all part of your **support network**. Friends, teachers, and community leaders are also there to talk to and **confide** in.

Absent but not forgotten

In most cases, parental absence is only temporary. Whether it is for a few weeks or months, most of the time there is an end date that marks the start of a family being back together. Remember that not seeing people does not mean you do not think of them or that they are not thinking of you. There are lots of different ways to see and talk to parents while they are away.

No matter what your situation or experience, you are not alone. Thousands of children all over the world are coping with absent parents in all kinds of different ways, and you, too, will find ways to cope and be happy.

Family and friends are there to support you and help you cope.

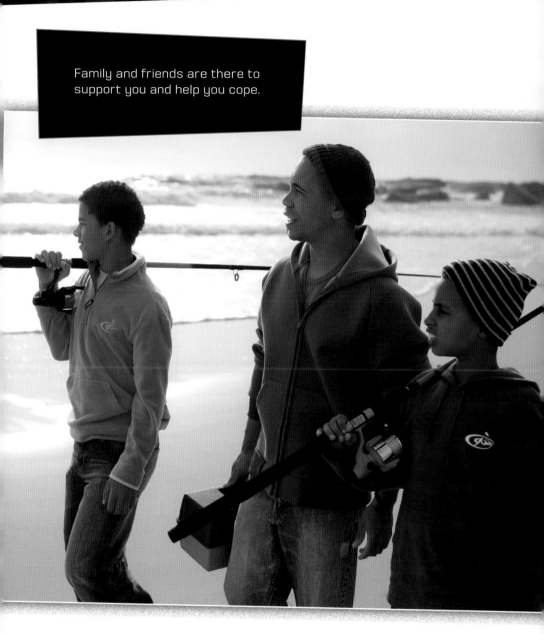

Top Ten Tips for Coping with Absent Parents

If your parents are absent for any reason, you might feel helpless. Here is a list of things to remember to help you cope:

1. Talk about how you feel with your friends, a grandparent, or another relative. Teachers and **counselors** are good to talk to, too. You will be amazed at how much better you will feel after sharing your emotions.

2. It's okay to cry if you are missing your parents. You will feel better afterward.

3. Keeping busy and joining in with your friends will stop you from dwelling on sad thoughts.

4. If you like a particular sport, there may be a team nearby you could join. Being involved in an activity is a good way to cope.

5. Ask a trusted adult to help you safely search the Internet to find advice websites. There is a lot of support out there.

6. Make a calendar and cross the days off until your mom or dad comes home.

7. If you are feeling lonely, don't stay inside. Get out on your bike or play out in the park.

8. Plan a variety of activities for when your parent is home again. These plans will give you something to look forward to.

9. Sharing your thoughts and feelings in a blog will encourage others to do the same, and you will have started an online **support network**.

10. Remember TEST: Text, Email, **Skype**, Tweet. These are all easy ways to keep in touch when your parent is away.

Coping with issues isn't easy, but it is possible to find new ways to be happy.

Glossary

abroad in a different country

adopted raised by parents who are not your birth parents, after a legal ruling

asylum seeking shelter and protection from danger in another country

confide tell someone something secret

cost of living amount of money spent on food, clothing, housing, and other basics needs

counseling support from someone who is trained to listen to and advise people who need help with problems

counselor person who is trained to listen to and advise people who need help with problems

culture beliefs, values, and traditions of a people or country

custody legal right to take care of a child

financial to do with money

foster care care given by people who are not your biological parents

gambling betting money

legally binding agreement or arrangement that must be kept to avoid breaking the law

mediator someone who works with people to reach an agreement

mentoring advising and supporting

migrant worker worker who travels in order to find work

oath of allegiance formal promise made by military personnel to be loyal to their country

on call ready to go to work at a moment's notice

paid leave paid time away from work

persecution being treated cruelly or unfairly because of your race or your religious or political beliefs

shift work period

Skype computer software that allows you to make video calls over the Internet

social networking site website, such as Facebook, Twitter, and MySpace, that brings together online groups of people who share interests

social worker care worker who helps people in need

support network people who care about you, such as your family, friends, and teachers

tour of duty period of military duty, usually for a fixed length of time

vulnerable at risk of being harmed physically or emotionally

Find Out More

Books

Cadier, Florence, and Melissa Daly. *My Parents Are Getting Divorced: How to Keep It Together When Your Mom and Dad Are Splitting Up.* New York: Amulet, 2004.

Guillain, Charlotte. *Coping with Moving Away (Real Life Issues).* Chicago: Heinemann Library, 2011.

Levete, Sarah. *Fostering and Adoption (Let's Talk About).* Mankato, Minn.: Stargazer, 2007.

Miles, Liz. *Coping with Illness (Real Life Issues).* Chicago: Heinemann LIbrary, 2011.

Weissmann, Joe. *Can I Catch It Like a Cold? Coping with a Parent's Depression.* Toronto: Tundra, 2009.

Websites and organizations

The following websites and organizations can offer help and support to you and your family:

Big Brothers Big Sisters
www.bbbsi.org
Big Brothers Big Sisters is a mentoring organization that helps children from 6 to 18 years old. Children are given a mentor to support them and help them through difficult times.

Foster Club
www.fosterclub.com
Foster Club is a national network for young people in foster care. Use this website to learn the stories of people who have experienced being in foster care.

Kids in the Middle

www.kidsinthemiddle.org

Kids in the Middle is an organization that helps children and parents dealing with divorce. There are links to different sections, depending on your age and situation.

Childhelp

www.childhelp.org

Tel: 1-800-4-A-CHILD

Childhelp helps children who have been neglected or abused. There is a helpline where you can talk to counselors 24 hours a day, 7 days a week.

American Association of Caregiving Youth

www.aacy.org

The American Association of Caregiving Youth is a group supporting young caregivers in the United States. The website is packed with helpful information, advice, support, and recreational activities designed to give young carers time out. There are also forums where you can express your thoughts.

National Association for Children of Alcoholics (Nacoa)

www.nacoa.org

The National Association for Children of Alcoholics can offer advice and support if your parent has a drinking problem.

The United States Committee for Refugees and Immigrants

www.refugees.org

The U.S. Committee for Refugees and Immigrants has a national center for child refugees who arrive on their own in the United States.

Index